THROUGH YOUR EYES

MY CHILD'S GIFT TO ME

Ainsley Earhardt

Through

YOUR EYES

MY CHILD'S GIFT TO ME

ILLUSTRATED BY JI-HYUK KIM

ALADDIN   New York   London   Toronto   Sydney   New Delhi

The moment we met
I wrote down a list
Of all we would do
Of what not to miss.

We'd soar through the skies
On a super-fast plane
Speed past snowy hills
On a passenger train.

But on a trip to the park
You opened my eyes
Taught me life is a gift
Every day a surprise.

You spread your arms wide
Near a starling of blue
Leaping into the air
Head back, you flew.

You built mountains from sand
Played tag with a tree
Who would have guessed
You could teach me to see?

Squealing with joy
When you spotted a dog
Eyes smiling with wonder
At the croak of a frog.

You smelled every tulip
Gentle beauty so real
Who would have thought
You could teach me to feel.

To slow down, take small steps
Make each moment last
The world is a blur
If you're spinning too fast.

The moment we met
I drew up a plan
To show you the world
To touch all you can.

Then you chased the wind
Whispered songs to the squirrels
Sitting still in the sun
Head bowed, soft curls.

Staring into the lake
You giggled with glee
Who would have known
You could teach me to be?

You danced in the puddles
When the rain pattered down
First we waltzed, then we sang
What a heavenly sound.

You counted the clouds
My heart pressed to your ear
Who would have known
You could teach me to hear?

To slow down, take small steps
Make each moment last
The world is a blur
If you're spinning too fast.

The moment we met
I wrote down a list
Of all we would do
Of what not to miss.

But when you took my hand
My list fluttered away
For the world through your eyes
Shines brand-new every day.

To our beautiful daughter, Hayden. What a gift from above!
Being your mother is my greatest joy. —A. E.

For my lovely wife and sweet daughter, who made my world a warmer place. —J. K.

"Start children off on the way they should go,
and even when they are old they will not turn from it." —Proverbs 22:6

THE STORY BEHIND THE STORY

On November 6, 2015, I delivered a baby, and my husband delivered the news to our waiting families: "It's a girl!"

Hayden DuBose Proctor was perfect and our hearts were full. She met all four of her amazing grandparents in the recovery room. Her little hands were perfectly wrapped around one finger of each grandfather, and my dad said, "How can anyone see a newborn baby and not believe in God?" It was a simple yet powerful and unforgettable moment for me. We were witnessing new life and a new generation.

During my pregnancy, I had so many hopes and dreams for Hayden: good health, a heart for others, love of God, righteousness, smarts, and happiness. I wanted to work even harder to give her the best life and make sure she was loved and protected every day. I hoped, and . . . I worried. I worried about being a good mother, teaching her, and making sure I could give her the brightest future. But the beauty and gift of being a parent is you learn quickly that you are not in control.

My daughter is *my* teacher. She is the one who helps me slow down and find wonder in the small things. I get the pleasure of watching a young human being discover life. For example, I will never forget when Hayden saw a dog for the first time. She squealed in excitement and loved the sweet animal immediately. Or the first time she saw rain. I watched her in awe as she stared in silence at the water dripping down in front of her stroller.

Each time she has a new experience, I do as well—through her eyes.

Hayden has taught me to enjoy every moment of this incredible life and not worry so much. She reminds me that this is not a dress rehearsal; time passes quickly and we only get one shot. I hope *Through Your Eyes* reminds you to treasure every moment of this glorious time on earth.

The author is donating a portion of her advance and of any subsequent royalties (in each case net of agency fees) to Folds of Honor, an organization that provides scholarships and assistance to the spouses and children of fallen soldiers in service to America. Learn more at foldsofhonor.org.

ALADDIN · An imprint of Simon & Schuster Children's Publishing Division · 1230 Avenue of the Americas, New York, New York 10020 · First Aladdin hardcover edition October 2017 · Text copyright © 2017 by Ainsley Proctor · Illustrations copyright © 2017 by Ji-Hyuk Kim · All rights reserved, including the right of reproduction in whole or in part in any form. · ALADDIN and related logo are registered trademarks of Simon & Schuster, Inc. · For information about special discounts for bulk purchases, please contact Simon & Schuster Special Sales at 1-866-506-1949 or business@simonandschuster.com. · The Simon & Schuster Speakers Bureau can bring authors to your live event. For more information or to book an event contact the Simon & Schuster Speakers Bureau at 1-866-248-3049 or visit our website at www.simonspeakers.com. · Designed by Jessica Handelman · The illustrations for this book were rendered in watercolor and digitally. · The text of this book was set in MrsEaves. · Manufactured in the United States of America 0917 PCH · 10 9 8 7 6 5 4 3 2 1 Library of Congress Control Number 2017938903 · ISBN 978-1-5344-0959-0 (hc) · ISBN 978-1-5344-0960-6 (eBook)